Copyright © 2000 by A.E.T. Browne and Partners
All rights reserved
First published in Great Britain by Doubleday,
a division of Transworld Publishers, 2000
Printed in Italy
Designed by Ian Butterworth
First American edition, 2001
3 5 7 9 10 8 6 4

Library of Congress Cataloging-in-Publication Data
Browne, Anthony.
    My dad / Anthony Browne — 1st American ed.
      p. cm.
    Summary: A child describes the many wonderful things about
"my dad," who can jump over the moon, swim like a fish, and
be as warm as toast.
    ISBN 0-374-35101-5
    [1. Fathers—Fiction.] 1. Title.
PZ7.B81984 My 2001
[E]
                                                                    00-37951

My Dad
Anthony Browne

F a r r a r   S t r a u s   G i r o u x

New York

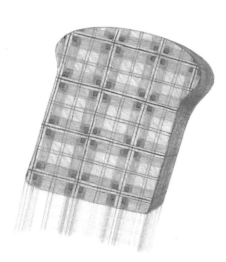

He's all right, my dad.

My dad isn't afraid of ANYTHING,

even the Big Bad Wolf.

He can jump right over the moon,

and walk on a tightrope (without falling off).

He can wrestle with giants,

or win the   fathers' race on
                    sports day, easily.

He's all right, my dad.

My dad can eat like a horse,

and he can swim like a fish.

He's as strong as a gorilla,

and as happy as a hippopotamus.

He's all right, my dad.

My dad's as big as a house,

and as soft as my teddy.

except when  he tries to help.

He's all right, my dad.

My dad's a great dancer,

and a brilliant singer.

He's fantastic at soccer,

and he makes me laugh. A lot.

I love my dad.
And you know what?

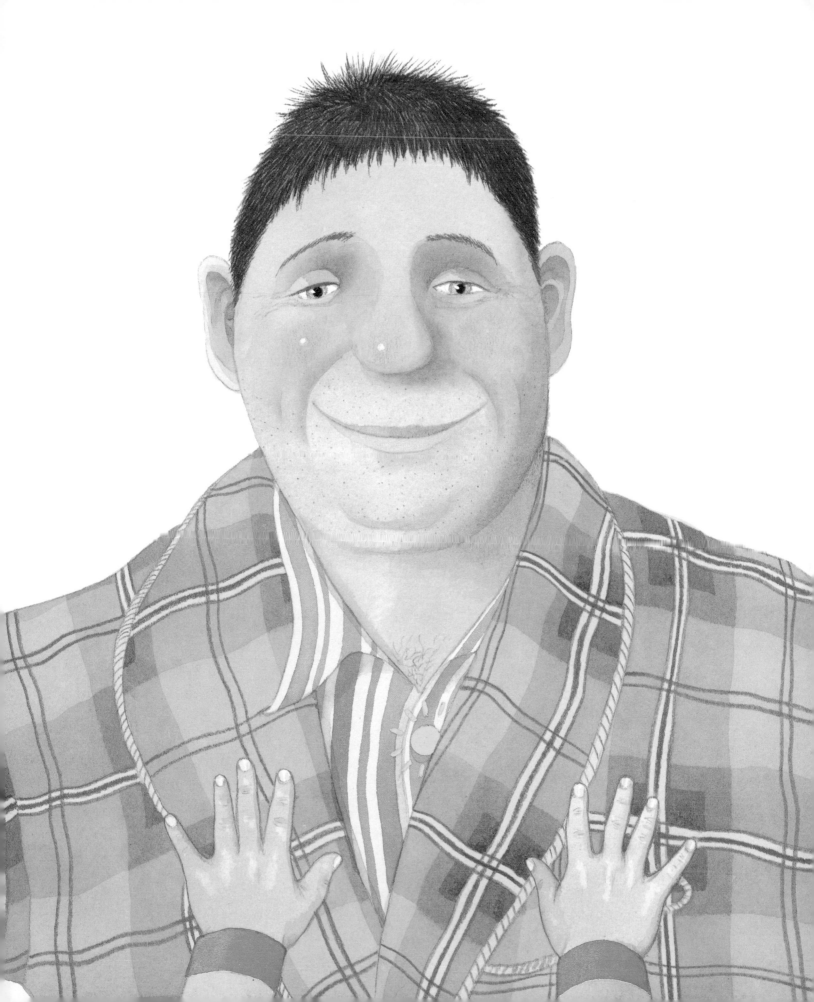

HE LOVES ME!

(And he always will.)